Edmund and the White Witch

Adapted from

The Chronicles of Narnia

by C. S. Lewis

Illustrated by Deborah Maze

HarperCollins*Publishers*

A special thanks to Douglas Gresham and the C. S. Lewis Estate
for their invaluable guidance and advice in helping to create
THE WORLD OF NARNIA picture books.

Library of Congress Cataloging-in-Publication Data
Edmund and the White Witch / adapted from the chronicles of
Narnia by C. S. Lewis ; illustrated by Deborah Maze.
    p.   cm.
   Summary: A boy finds his way through the back of a wardrobe
into the magic land of Narnia and meets the White Witch who
feeds him enchanted Turkish Delight.
   ISBN 0-06-027516-2. — ISBN 0-06-027517-0 (lib. bdg.)
   [1. Fantasy.]   I. Lewis, C. S. (Clive Staples), 1898–1963. Chronicles
of Narnia. II. Maze, Deborah, ill.
PZ7.E2465 1997   96-23202
[E]—dc20   CIP
                                          AC

Typography by Steve Scott
2 3 4 5 6 7 8 9 10
❖

To John, Jenny, and Chris, with love
—D. M.

Long ago in the city of London, during the Second World War, there were four children whose names were Peter, Susan, Edmund, and Lucy. Because of the air-raids they were sent far into the country to stay at the big old house of Professor Kirke. This is the story of their adventure.

The house was a large house, and it was full of unexpected places. One room was entirely empty except for a big wardrobe with a looking-glass on the door. On the very first day the children explored the house, Lucy stepped through the wardrobe into Narnia, a wondrous snowy land full of curious creatures. There she had a marvelous tea with Mr. Tumnus, a Faun, who told her all about Narnia and the terrible White Witch who had made it always winter and never Christmas.

When Lucy jumped back out of the wardrobe, she hurried to find her brothers and sister to tell them about her adventure. But they thought she was making up the whole story. And when Lucy showed them the wardrobe, all they saw was an ordinary wardrobe with an ordinary back to it.

So their adventures in Narnia might have ended forever, except that on the next rainy day, while playing hide-and-seek, Lucy went to hide in the wardrobe and found herself back in Narnia. Wanting to tease her, Edmund followed her into the wardrobe, and much to his surprise he too found himself in the snowy wood. Lucy was nowhere to be seen, and everything was perfectly still, as if he were the only living creature around.

Suddenly Edmund heard a sound of bells. The sound came nearer and nearer and at last there swept into sight a sledge drawn by two reindeer. They were white with gilded horns, and their scarlet harness was covered with bells. A fat dwarf sat on the sledge driving the reindeer, and behind him sat a great lady, taller and more beautiful than any woman Edmund had ever seen. She was covered in white fur up to her throat, and she held a long straight golden wand in her right hand and wore a golden crown on her head.

"Stop!" said the Lady. "And what, pray, are you?" she said, looking at Edmund.

"I—I'm—my name's Edmund," said Edmund.

The Lady frowned. "Is that how you address a Queen?" she asked.

"I beg your pardon, your Majesty, I didn't know," said Edmund.

"Not know the Queen of Narnia?" she cried. "Ha! You shall know us better hereafter. But I repeat, what are you?"

"I'm a boy, your Majesty," answered Edmund.

"A Son of Adam? You mean you are Human?"

"Yes, your Majesty."

"And how, pray, did you come to enter my dominions?"

"Please, your Majesty, I opened a door and just found myself here," said Edmund.

"Ha!" said the Queen. "A door from the world of men. I have heard of such things. This may wreck all." She rose from her seat and raised her wand. Edmund felt sure that she was going to do something dreadful.

But then the Queen sat down again and said gently, "My poor child, how cold you look! Come and sit with me and we will talk."

Edmund dared not disobey. So he stepped onto the sledge and sat at her feet, and she put a fold of her fur mantle around him and tucked it well in.

"Perhaps you would like something hot to drink?" said the Queen.

"Yes please, your Majesty," said Edmund, whose teeth were chattering.

The Queen took out a small bottle, and she let a single drop fall onto the snow below. There was a hissing sound and there stood a jeweled cup full of something that steamed. The dwarf handed the cup to Edmund, who took a sip. It was something he had never tasted before, very sweet and foamy and creamy, and it warmed him right down to his toes.

"It is dull, Son of Adam, to drink without eating," said the Queen. "What would you like best to eat?"

"Turkish Delight, please, your Majesty," said Edmund.

The Queen let another drop fall from her bottle, and instantly there appeared a round box, tied with green silk ribbon and full of the best Turkish Delight Edmund had ever tasted.

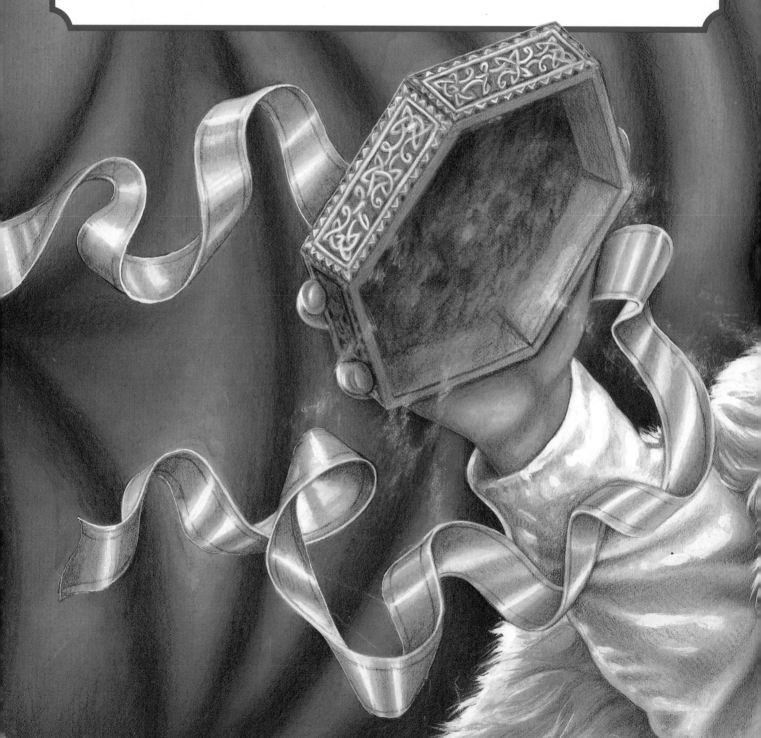

Edmund was quite warm now, and very comfortable. While he was eating, the Queen kept asking questions. Edmund spoke with his mouth full of Turkish Delight and kept forgetting to say "Your Majesty," but she didn't seem to mind now. She got him to tell her that he had one brother and two sisters, and that one of his sisters had already been in Narnia and had met a Faun there.

At last the Turkish Delight was finished. Edmund wished that the Queen would ask him whether he would like some more. In fact, Edmund did not know that this was enchanted Turkish Delight, and that anyone who tasted it would want more and more of it.

But the Queen did not offer him any more. Instead, she said to him, "Son of Adam, I should so much like to see your brother and your two sisters. Will you bring them to see me?"

"I'll try," said Edmund, looking at the empty box of candy.

"Because if you did come again—with your brother and sisters, of course—I'd be able to give you some more Turkish Delight. In my own house, there are whole rooms of Turkish Delight! And what's more, I have no children of my own. I want a nice boy whom I could bring up to be King of Narnia when I am gone. While he was Prince he would wear a gold crown and eat Turkish Delight all day long. I think I would like to make you the Prince—some day, when you bring the others to visit me. So you must go back to your own country now and bring them to me. It's no good coming without them."

The Queen pointed with her wand. "Next time you come you have only to look for those two hills rising above the trees and walk toward them until you reach my house. But remember—you must bring the others with you. I might have to be very angry with you if you came alone."

"I'll do my best," said Edmund.

"And, by the way," said the Queen as Edmund climbed out of the sledge, "you needn't tell them about me. It would be fun to keep it a secret between us two, wouldn't it? If your sister has met one of the Fauns, she may have heard nasty stories about me. Fauns will say anything, you know. . . ."

The sledge swept away out of sight.

Edmund was still staring after the sledge when he heard someone calling his name. Looking around he saw Lucy coming toward him from another part of the wood.

"Oh, Edmund!" she cried. "So you've got in too!"

"All right," said Edmund. "It is a magic wardrobe after all. But where on earth have you been?"

"I've been having lunch with Mr. Tumnus, and he's very well. The White Witch has done nothing to him for letting me go when I had tea with him before, so he thinks she can't have found out," answered Lucy.

"The White Witch?" said Edmund. "Who's she?"

"She's a perfectly terrible person," said Lucy. "Mr. Tumnus told me all about her. She calls herself the Queen of Narnia though she has no right to be queen at all, and everyone hates her. She can turn people into stone and do all kinds of terrible things. She drives about on a sledge, drawn by reindeer, with a wand in her hand and a crown on her head."

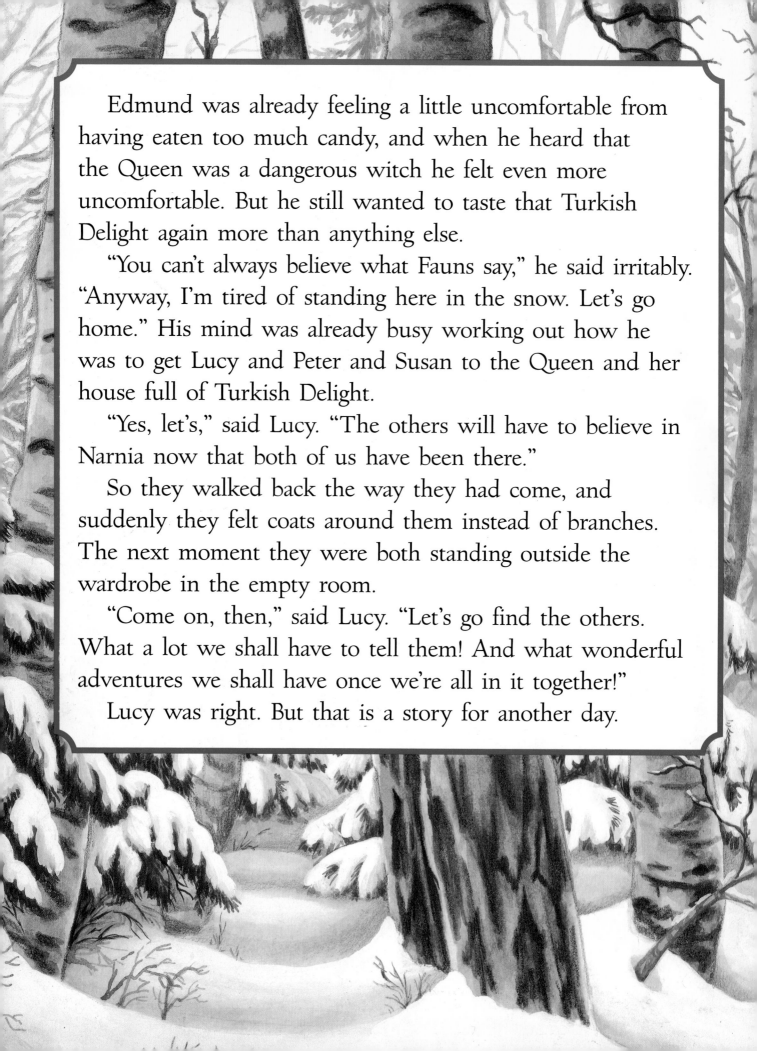

Edmund was already feeling a little uncomfortable from having eaten too much candy, and when he heard that the Queen was a dangerous witch he felt even more uncomfortable. But he still wanted to taste that Turkish Delight again more than anything else.

"You can't always believe what Fauns say," he said irritably. "Anyway, I'm tired of standing here in the snow. Let's go home." His mind was already busy working out how he was to get Lucy and Peter and Susan to the Queen and her house full of Turkish Delight.

"Yes, let's," said Lucy. "The others will have to believe in Narnia now that both of us have been there."

So they walked back the way they had come, and suddenly they felt coats around them instead of branches. The next moment they were both standing outside the wardrobe in the empty room.

"Come on, then," said Lucy. "Let's go find the others. What a lot we shall have to tell them! And what wonderful adventures we shall have once we're all in it together!"

Lucy was right. But that is a story for another day.